AMBER'S WHOLE WORLD IS CHANGING.

I, Amber Brown, used to live in a house. I went away for a night and a day and while I was gone, Mom and Max turned the place into a disaster zone.

They have filled our home with boxes. There are boxes everywhere. Boxes for the books.....boxes for the dishes.....boxes for the glasses.....boxes for the towels. I know what they are for because Max has labeled each one with a Magic Marker.

He has also numbered them.

Walking between all the boxes makes me feel like a mouse in a maze.

I look into what used to be the living room. There are no pictures on the walls, no books on the shelves, no knickknacks on the end tables.

I look around the room at all the boxes.

"I don't want to move. I love this house."

OTHER BOOKS YOU MAY ENJOY

AMBER BROWN

IS ON THE MOVE

Paula Danziger's

written by Bruce Coville
and Elizabeth Levy
illustrations by Anthony Lewis

PUFFIN BOOKS
An Imprint of Penguin Group (USA)

PUFFIN BOOKS
Published by the Penguin Group
Penguin Group (USA) LLC
375 Hudson Street
New York, New York 10014

USA ★ Canada ★ UK ★ Ireland ★ Australia
New Zealand ★ India ★ South Africa ★ China

penguin.com
A Penguin Random House Company

First published in the United States of America by G. P. Putnam's Sons,
an imprint of Penguin Young Readers Group, 2013
Published by Puffin Books, an imprint of Penguin Young Readers Group, 2014

THE LIBRARY OF CONGRESS HAS CATALOGED THE G. P. PUTNAM SON'S EDITION AS FOLLOWS:
Coville, Bruce.
Paula Danziger's Amber Brown is on the move / written by Bruce Coville
and Elizabeth Levy ; interior illustrations by Anthony Lewis.
p. cm.
Summary: "Now that Amber's mom and Max are married, the family is moving to a new
house, and Amber is worried about more than just packing. How can she leave the
only home she's ever known?"—Provided by publisher.
ISBN 978-0-399-16169-8 (hc)
[1. Moving, Household—Fiction. 2. Family life—Fiction. 3. Schools—Fiction.]
I. Levy, Elizabeth, date– II. Lewis, Anthony, date– illustrator. III. Danziger, Paula, 1944–2004.
IV. Title. V. Title: Amber Brown is on the move.
PZ7.C8344Pas 2013
[Fic]—dc23
2013012631

Puffin Books ISBN 978-0-14-751223-9

Printed in the United States of America

Design by Annie Ericsson

3 5 7 9 10 8 6 4 2

To Emilyn Garrick, Dinah Krosnick,
Paul Smith, and all the kids at the
Bronx New School, who showed us
how much they love to dance,
and with special thanks to Pierre Dulaine,
who created Dancing Classrooms.

Chapter One

I, Amber Brown, am not amused. My mother has just put a big box in my room and told me to fill it.

It should be easy to fill the box because my room has tons of stuff. The problem is, Mom has labeled the box AMBER'S TOYS TO DONATE.

This is not for some holiday toy drive.

This is not because there has been a disaster, and Mom wants to send some of my toys to needy children.

This is because we are moving.

Right now, Mom is standing in my

doorway staring at the empty box. She does that a lot lately. "Amber," she says, "you've got to get started. I don't want to bring all this clutter to our new house."

"This isn't clutter," I tell her. "This is my life."

"Moving house is the best time for cleaning out old junk," Mom says. "It's time for a fresh start."

That may be true, but a lot of what Mom calls old junk has good memories attached to it. Most of those memories have to do with when Dad still lived here, which I like thinking of . . . . . but Mom does not.

For example, there's the couch. Mom and Dad and I used to cuddle up on it every Sunday night to watch a movie. I'll admit it's kind of beat-up and it's got some glitter glued to it . . . . all right, a lot of glitter. Even so, I'm really going to miss it.

And it's not just big things, like the couch. Mom wants me to get rid of a lot of MY things!

I look at the box again.

I would like to fill it with crumpled-up newspapers, but I don't think Mom will accept that.

In my opinion, I, Amber Brown, should never have to move. But I don't have much choice. Next week Mom and Max and I are heading for our new house.

Actually, Max moved in with us right after he and Mom got married. But that was only temporary because we had already bought the new house. At least it's in the same town, so I don't have to change schools.

The thing was, we had to wait for it to be ready. So Max moved in here. Now, just a few weeks later, we're moving out.

We're taking Max with us, of course.

Moving is hard work . . . . . and it's

even harder on your brain than it is on your body. Big changes are a big pain on the brain. But one thing I, Amber Brown, have learned in nine and three-quarters years is that things are going to change whether I want them to or not.

I didn't really want a new house. I like this one just fine. But Mom and Max bought one anyway.

I didn't want a new life. But Mom and Dad divorced anyway.

I didn't want a new best friend. But my best friend ever, Justin Daniels, moved anyway.

Actually, Justin is still my best friend, but I have two new best friends, Kelly Green and Brandi Colwin. I know "best" is supposed to mean only one . . . . . but I think that's a silly rule.

I look at the box again. Maybe I should just put myself in it and mail it to Alabama, where Justin and his family live.

But what would I do if I had to pee before the box was delivered? I don't think even Express Mail goes that fast.

I decide I should call Justin instead.

I go to ask if it's okay.

Mom and Max are in the kitchen. Mom is holding up a plate.

Max says, "I have a complete set of china too, and none of it is chipped."

Mom doesn't look happy. "But these were my mother's. Besides, Amber grew up with them."

Mom is right. I have been eating off those plates all my life. I don't want different ones. But maybe Max wants his own plates too.

I realize Mom and Max are also going to have to get rid of a lot of their stuff. Trying to squeeze two houses' worth of things into one new house would probably make the place explode . . . . . or at least it would make our heads explode.

I also realize that Mom and Max are not having fun either. I decide I don't want to be in this kitchen right now.

"Mom," I say. "I need to call Justin."

"Go ahead," she answers.

I turn around and run upstairs. Mom never lets me call Justin without a small fuss first and I want to do it before she can change her mind.

Mrs. Daniels answers the phone. "Hi, Amber," she says cheerfully. "How's the move going?"

"I think it's going to move me to tears," I say. "Mom and Max aren't doing so well either."

"Oh, honey, I remember how hard it is. Moving is no picnic. I'll give your mom and Max a call later. Justin is right here."

Justin gets on the phone. "You almost got an Express Mail package," I tell him.

"You're not going to send back the chewing gum ball, are you?"

When Justin and I were little, we started making a ball from our used chewing gum. When Justin moved, he left it in my custody. It's lived in my closet ever since. Justin still sends used gum to add to it from time to time. He says it helps us stick together.

"Actually, I was thinking of sending myself," I tell him.

"What would you do when you had to pee?"

"That's why I changed my mind. I decided to just call you instead. I'm ready to pack it in on this packing, and I haven't even started yet."

"Let me guess. Your mother is going to make you throw stuff away."

"How did you know?"

"Because I had to do the same thing when we moved. I hated it, but it was mostly little kid stuff. I don't miss any of it now."

"This is not helping," I say.

"It's just stuff, Amber."

I do not like hearing that the things I love are just stuff.

When I was little and said something silly, Aunt Pam would laugh and say, "Oh, stuff and nonsense." But my stuff is not nonsense. It's my stuff, and I love it.

After Justin and I hang up, I sit on my bed and pick up Gorilla. He is a stuffed toy that Dad won for me at the town fair. He is not going into that box.

I need him to talk to.

"You may be stuffed, but you are not just stuff," I tell him.

He doesn't answer.

I look around my room.

I don't see one single thing that I want to put in that stupid box.

Chapter Two

When I get to school on Monday, I am still cranky . . . . . or at least on the edge of cranky and in danger of falling off.

Mrs. Holt, however, is grinning. "I have a wonderful announcement," she says.

"No practice test today!" Jimmy Russell shouts.

"No tests at all!" Bobby Clifford shouts.

Mrs. Holt's grin gets a little tight and she says, "Be careful, boys, or I might decide to have two practice tests today."

Bobby and Jimmy cover their mouths with their hands.

Lately school has been about as much fun as packing. That's because statewide testing is in a few weeks. Mrs. Holt and our principal, Mr. Robinson, have made it clear that doing well on the statewide tests is REALLY IMPORTANT.

"Here's the news. Our class has been accepted for a special program where you fourth graders will learn ballroom dancing. A professional dancer will come in on Mondays and Fridays to teach you."

Hal Henry, whose big ears have turned bright red, falls off his chair.

Most of the other boys look like they want to crawl under their desks. Some of the girls do too. But I remember Mom and Max's wedding and their first dance. It was a waltz, and it was beautiful. I really wished I knew how to do it.

"No way am I doing ballroom dancing!" Bobby shouts.

"That's the goofiest idea I ever heard!" Jimmy cries.

"That's enough, boys," Mrs. Holt says. She is not mad, but I can tell she is very serious. "This program has been used in over two hundred schools, and at the beginning the kids are always nervous or upset. But every single time when it is over, everyone has loved it and asks to do it again the next year. So I want you to stop fussing and give it a chance. We have been together for almost a year now, and I hope you know that you can trust me when I tell you something like this."

She looks around. No one says anything for a minute. Then Fredrich Allen, who has a major nose-picking problem, but who I have learned is nicer than I thought, raises his hand. I am happy to see that his fingers are booger-free.

"I know how to dance," he says. "I had

to learn because of my dad's camp. It's actually kind of fun."

Bobby Clifford sticks his finger in his mouth like he wants to throw up. For some reason the more Bobby doesn't like Fredrich, the more I do.

Then Hannah Burton raises her hand. "Does this mean we should wear special outfits on Mondays and Fridays?" she simpers.

I just learned that word, *simpers*, last week. It means to smile or speak in a silly, fake manner. I was really happy when I found it because it's a perfect description of how Hannah talks.

The boys groan again.

"No, Hannah, not until the final dance contest," Mrs. Holt tells her.

"Contest?" Hannah asks. I can tell that she is thinking about what to say in her winner's speech.

"Yes. We will be competing with five different schools."

"How can we have a contest the same time we have the state tests?" Kelly asks.

"We won't," Mrs. Holt says. "The contest doesn't happen until testing is over. As for the dance lessons, when I went to Mr. Robinson to get permission, he agreed it would be a good way for us to let off some steam. He knows that we're all under a lot of pressure right now."

Someone knocks on the door. Before Mrs. Holt can answer, it swings open and Mr. Robinson steps in.

Beside him is a tall woman with long red hair. She must be the dance teacher. First of all, she's in high heels, which almost none of our teachers wear. Second, she's carrying a shoulder bag that says MOVE AND GROOVE DANCE STUDIO. Third, she is wearing a black leotard and a skirt

that looks like layers and layers of butterfly wings. She makes me feel like a caterpillar. She is not really beautiful, but for some reason I can't take my eyes off her.

"Good morning, class," Mr. Robinson says. "Allow me to present Miss Isobel Godwin. She's going to be your dance instructor."

Miss Godwin makes a deep curtsy. If I tried to do that, I'm pretty sure I would fall over. "You may call me Miss Isobel." She has a slight accent, but I can't tell where it's from. "I'm very pleased to meet you, ladies and gentlemen."

I glance around to see how the boys react to the word *gentlemen*. They're just staring at Miss Isobel. Bobby Clifford's face has turned as red as Hal Henry's ears.

Mr. Robinson nods at Mrs. Holt. She claps and says, "Move your desks to pattern C."

We've done this lots of times. We get

up and slide our desks to the sides of the room, which leaves a big space in the center.

Miss Isobel and Mr. Robinson move to the middle of the room. Miss Isobel nods to Mrs. Holt, who presses a button on the computer.

The music begins.

"Dance hold!" Miss Isobel says.

Mr. Robinson raises his arms and Miss Isobel steps toward him. "Mr. Robinson has been practicing with me. We will now show you the tango and the swing."

Mr. Robinson puts his left hand on her waist. They put their right hands together at about shoulder height. They begin to dance.

I have never seen Mr. Robinson stand up so straight. "T-A-N-G-O!" Miss Isobel calls, pronouncing each letter in time to the music. They glide across the floor. I am amazed. Mr. Robinson has moves!

Or maybe it's just that Miss Isobel makes him look like a great dancer.

Suddenly the music changes. "Swing!" Miss Isobel shouts. They begin waving their hands in the air and shaking their hips.

The first dance looked very grown-up. This one looks like pure fun.

"I've never seen Mr. Robinson grin so much," I whisper to Kelly, who is sitting next to me.

"He's not grinning, he's drooling over the dance teacher!" she answers.

When they are done, Mr. Robinson bows to Miss Isobel and then to us. We all applaud.

Miss Isobel says, "When we meet on Friday, I will assign partners. I will do this based on height, as I want the pairs to look good. You will be learning the two dances Mr. Robinson and I just showed you—tango and swing. In addition you will learn the fox trot and the waltz. When we are done, you will have a skill you will enjoy for the rest of your life. Because here is a simple truth: The better you can dance, the more comfortable you are with dancing, the more fun life is. We were born to dance!"

She curtsies again and heads for the door. Her butterfly skirt swirls around her as she moves. Mr. Robinson hurries to the door and opens it for her with a flourish.

"Mrs. Holt, are you going to dance too?" Fredrich asks.

She smiles. "I might."

I have a hard time focusing on my work for the rest of the morning. I keep thinking about dancing instead. When we go out for recess, the girls get together to figure out how tall everyone is and who we might end up with. I had a growth spurt in October, so I am pretty sure I am taller than Bobby and Jimmy, which is a relief. I might be the same size as Gregory Gifford. Gregory is fun . . . . . he can burp the alphabet. But that doesn't mean he has rhythm.

The girls are all excited, and a little scared.

The boys just look scared.

After recess we do another practice test. I think it might be more fun to hit myself on the head with a baseball bat. No matter how scary dancing might be, it has to be better than this. I am starting to get excited about the dance lessons. Soon I am daydreaming about winning the trophy.

As we get ready to leave school, I feel a bubble of happiness dancing inside me.

Then Mrs. Holt says, "Amber, I need to talk to you."

My happy bubble pops.

Chapter Three

I, Amber Brown, am sitting in the principal's office.

So is my mother.

So is my father.

So is Max.

And so is Mrs. Holt.

None of us are happy campers. Mrs. Holt has called this meeting because I am not doing well on the state practice tests. That was what she told me after school two days ago . . . . . that she had e-mailed my parents to come in for a meeting with her and Mr. Robinson.

As if my test scores weren't bad enough, her e-mail created a new problem: Who should come to the meeting? Max is now my official stepfather. Dad is still my dad. They don't get along that well. This is mostly because Dad still has a hard time with Mom being married again. It's even worse now that Max is living in what used to be Dad's house, even if it's only until we move.

Despite all this, Mom felt they should both be at the meeting.

"Dad is your dad," she told me, "and he has to be there. But you spend most of the week with me and Max, so he needs to be there too."

She sent me out of the room when she called Dad to talk about it. Even from upstairs I could tell that it was not a happy conversation.

Max looks so worried that I wonder if

this is the first time he ever had to go the principal's office. Maybe he was a perfect kid. Or maybe it's because, until me, he never had a kid of his own. I'm sure not perfect.

"Does this mean that Amber won't go on to fifth grade?" he asks Mr. Robinson.

Mr. Robinson shakes his head. "We are getting ahead of ourselves, Mr. Turner. Our goal today is to help Amber focus so she can pass the tests."

"I know Amber can handle the material," Mrs. Holt says. "She just doesn't seem to focus."

I shrink back in my seat. I wish this wasn't true, but it is. What with all the planning for the wedding and then all the fuss about moving, I've had a lot on my mind this spring.

Looking straight at me, Mrs. Holt says, "Your test scores are way below where they should be, Amber. I know you can do better. Much better."

I like Mrs. Holt, but I know what she means. Right now, I'm taking a nose dive to the bottom of the aquarium.

Then Dad makes things even worse.

"I don't think it's entirely Amber's fault," he says. "She's had a lot of distractions at her mother's home lately."

Mom's face turns red. I can't tell if she's embarrassed or furious. What I can tell is that she wishes she hadn't made that phone call to Dad.

Max gets a look on his face that makes me think that if he and Dad were ten years old, there would soon be a circle of kids around them shouting, "Fight! Fight!"

Mr. Robinson must see this too because he uses his principal-on-the-playground voice to say, "Let's focus on the issue at hand, which is actually Amber's focus . . . . . or more precisely, her lack of it."

Mom and Dad at least have been through this before. This is not the first time a teacher has said, "Amber loses focus."

You'd think everyone wants me to grow up to be a camera.

"We feel Amber should be enrolled in our Saturday Academy," Mr. Robinson says.

I groan. Saturday Academy is a program the district runs in April and May to help kids prepare for the state tests. I've stayed out of it so far, and I do not, do not, do not want to have to spend my Saturdays in school.

"I think that's a good idea," Dad says.

I glare at him. Saturday is the only whole day that I have with Dad. He usually picks me up from school on Friday afternoon. We go to his apartment. We hang out together all day Saturday. Then on Sunday he takes me back to Mom and Max.

"What happens if she still can't pass the test?" Max asks.

Now Dad and I both glare at him. I am having a hard time deciding who to be angry at.

"We don't get the results of the final tests until August," Mr. Robinson says.

28

"However, depending on how Amber's schoolwork and practice tests go between now and June, we may recommend that she get more help during the summer."

"I don't want more help!" I say, crossing my arms over my chest and sinking deeper into the chair. "I'm supposed to go to camp with Brandi and Kelly."

"Then I suggest you use your energy more wisely for the rest of the year," Mr. Robinson says sternly.

The first time I was in Mr. Robinson's office, I was upset and he helped me calm down. That was when he taught me how to drink cream soda through a chocolate Twizzler.

Now he is upset with me.

Everyone is upset with me.

Even I am upset with me.

What I really want to focus on right now is getting out of this room.

Instead, I, Amber Brown, am enrolled in Saturday Academy.

Maybe I should mail myself to Alabama after all. I'll just make sure to pack a bucket.

Chapter Four

Miss Isobel is standing in the middle of the multipurpose room or, as I like to call it, the cafetorinasium. It's after lunch, so the janitor has cleaned up . . . . which means that the room now smells like disinfectant mixed with a hint of broccoli.

We get a lot more vegetables at lunch than we used to. Sometimes they are mixed vegetables . . . . which I definitely have mixed feelings about. Tiffani Schroeder, on the other hand, is completely happy. That's because she's a vegetarian.

I would like to be a pizzatarian.

Miss Isobel is smiling. She gives us a little curtsy. "Ladies and gentlemen, please get into two lines. Ladies on my right, gentlemen on my left. Mrs. Holt, please help them line up by size, shortest to tallest."

This is the moment we've all been dreading . . . . . the moment when we discover who we will have to dance with.

I keep eying the other line to find out who I'll get. But Mrs. Holt won't stop

moving us around. Every time I think I've figured out my partner, she changes the line again. When she moves me ahead of two other girls, I am annoyed. I thought I was taller. I feel taller.

Kelly and Hannah are behind me. Brandi is right in front of me. Tiffani Schroeder is at the very front because she is the shortest. It's kind of odd that she's shortest because she's the only one of

us who needs a bra. I don't even need a training bra. I have nothing to put in it.

I realize I am losing my focus.

Miss Isobel claps. "Ladies and gentlemen, we will now have our first promenade. You will walk toward me. When a pair reaches me, the gentleman will bow to his partner and offer his arm."

Miss Isobel must have a very good imagination if she sees any gentlemen here. The boys are all looking as if they would rather lose an arm than offer one.

Miss Isobel turns to them. "Gentlemen, you need to understand the history and traditions of dance. The reason you offer your left arm is because in olden times, your right arm had to be free for your sword. Your job during the dance is to protect your partner and make her feel safe."

I expect the boys to fall on the floor giggling, but they are listening to her as if they can't wait to draw their swords and protect her.

"Now, gentlemen, stand up straight!"

They do.

"Show me your bows."

The boys bow. Every one of them ends up with his head at a different level. Miss Isobel laughs, but it is a pretty sound, not mocking. "This is a good start," she says. "However, I would like you to only go this far."

She demonstrates with a little bow, then says, "Now, try again."

It's startling. They actually do look like a line of gentlemen. Mrs. Holt looks astonished.

Miss Isobel turns to us girls. "Now, the bow . . . . the bow, it is easy. The curtsy, however . . . . . ah, that must be practiced if one is not to fall upon one's face."

She is not telling me something that I don't already know!

Then she does tell us something that I don't know: how to do it!

Demonstrating as she speaks, she says, "Put your right foot behind your left foot. Not up tight to the heel . . . . give yourself room! Now, briefly bend the knees . . . . just so . . . . and bow your head and shoulders slightly forward. Smile! That is most important! All right, now you try."

We try. Some of us are a bit wobbly, but no one falls over.

"Good, good. Now try again. Again! Ah, very good!"

It actually feels very good to hear her say that.

"And so, we begin. Music, please!"

A march begins. We are moving!

Tiffani and Eric pair up first. We could see that coming. Brandi, who is right in front of me, leans back and whispers, "I miscounted! I'm getting Fredrich."

And sure enough, when Fredrich gets

to Miss Isobel, he bows to Brandi and offers her his arm. I notice that he makes the best bow of any of the boys.

Brandi puts her hand on his elbow, which even Fredrich can't get into his nose.

I'm next and . . . . OMG! . . . . I'm getting Bobby!

Suddenly Fredrich looks very good, nose-picking or not. Bobby is the goofiest boy in our class. Or maybe the second goofiest. It's hard to tell from day to day who is worse, Bobby or Jimmy.

Mrs. Holt has always told us that everyone has a special talent, we just have to find it. Bobby has already found his . . . . he can make more different rude noises with his armpit than anyone else in the entire school.

I think about that when I have to put my hand on his left arm.

I trip when we are walking side by side. I don't know how that is Bobby's fault, and maybe it isn't. I just know this is going to be a nightmare.

"Stay in pairs and make a half circle around me," trills Miss Isobel.

This is when I realize that Roger Hart does not have a partner. Our class has always had more boys than girls, and since Roger is the tallest boy, he was at the end of the line. He looks upset.

Miss Isobel smiles at him. "Ah, I am delighted to have someone left, especially a boy. So often I must dance with a girl. You will be my assistant. What is your name, young man?"

Roger, who has never stammered before, stammers out his name.

Miss Isobel smiles. "Good. Roger, you will help me with my demonstrations. Also, during our lessons you will rotate as the alternate when someone is absent."

I try to imagine Roger dancing with Tiffani. He is so tall and she is so short that she would look like a peanut next to him. Except that wouldn't be allowed because we are a peanut-free school.

That makes me wish Hannah Burton was a peanut.

"Amber," Bobby says to me, "we're supposed to be facing each other."

I realize I hadn't heard what Miss Isobel just told us to do and Bobby did. Wow. If Bobby is paying attention and I'm not, maybe I really do have a problem with focus!

Miss Isobel says, "Today we will learn dance hold, but with pancake hands."

Bobby snickers. "Pancake hands should be easy for Fredrich. He already knows how to eat his finger."

I don't laugh. Bobby makes a face at me.

I think about what Miss Isobel said . . . . the gentleman should protect the lady. I wish someone would protect me from Bobby.

"Make your hands flat, as if they are pancakes," Miss Isobel tells us. "Lift them to shoulder height. Now place your palms gently against your partner's. Keep your elbows easy."

"Elbows easy" makes me think of macaroni, and pancakes make me think of, well, pancakes. But maybe that's because I don't want to think of touching Bobby. But I do. I put my flat hands against his.

Miss Isobel goes around the circle, adjusting people's arms and hands. When she comes to us, she touches Bobby's shoulders and says, "Straight and tall! A gentleman must show respect for his partner. You provide the frame for the lady. Think of her as a beautiful picture."

I expect Bobby to burst out laughing at the idea of me being beautiful, but he is listening to Miss Isobel more carefully than he has ever listened to Mrs. Holt.

Also, his mouth is hanging open.

I am afraid that in a minute I am going to have to tuck his tongue back in.

I hope this will not be one of my jobs as his partner.

When Miss Isobel has everyone standing the way she wants, she teaches us the box step.

"Don't we need music to do this?" Bobby asks.

Miss Isobel smiles. "First we learn the step, then we add the music."

This is harder than it sounds. I have to take a step backward while Bobby goes forward. Then we go to the side. The problem is, I keep starting with the wrong foot. Every time Miss Isobel says, "Ladies start on the right," I start on my left, and Bobby steps on my toes. The annoying thing is that not only does Bobby get it right, he's actually kind of nice to me.

He says, "Relax, Amber, you'll get it."

But Bobby is wrong. I don't get it. Then Miss Isobel starts the music, and it's even worse. . . . . I keep putting my feet in the wrong place and bumping into his. I'm afraid Bobby will get mad, but he laughs . . . . . and it's not a mean laugh. I can tell that he's having fun.

To my surprise, so am I.

I bet it would be really fun if I could manage to do it right. At the end of the dance Miss Isobel tells the gentlemen to bow to their partners and the girls to curtsy.

I am surprised to hear people applauding.

"And now," Miss Isobel says, "bow and curtsy to your audience."

When we turn toward the clapping, we see that several parents have been watching us. My dad is one of them. He is smiling. Even better, I can see that he is really proud of me.

That makes me happy.

Sometimes my dad can be a pain. Even so, I, Amber Brown, am glad that he is my dad. And always will be.

Chapter
Five

Dad and I walk to his new car. It is bright red and very sporty. Dad named it "the Hot Tamale."

Mom named it "Your father's middle-aged-man-starting-over car."

Sometimes I think it is no surprise my parents got divorced.

Dad says, "Amber, you looked so cute while you were dancing. I loved it."

I make a face. I didn't want to be cute, I wanted to be elegant. On the other hand, given how many times I stepped on Bobby's feet, I was closer to "elephant" than "elegant."

Dad's car is parked next to a green VW Bug. "Now, that's cute," I say, pointing to the little car.

"I am glad you like it," says a voice from behind us.

I turn around. It is Miss Isobel.

"You're the dance teacher," Dad says. "I thought what you were doing with the kids was great."

He is wearing the same goofy grin that Bobby did.

Miss Isobel smiles and nods modestly. "Thank you. And your daughter . . . . Opal, is it?"

"Amber," I say.

She waves her hand, flicking her fingers. "Names. I am not so good at names. It is how you move that I will remember.

Anyway, I was going to say, your daughter has a lovely smile."

I notice she does not say anything about my dancing.

She extends her hand to Dad. "I am Isobel Godwin."

I half expect her to curtsy. Dad looks like he wants to bow. Instead he just says, "I'm Philip Brown, Amber's father."

"And do you dance, father of Amber?"

Dad says that he loves to dance. This is news to me.

"You must visit my studio. I give adult lessons as well."

Miss Isobel digs in her purse, then hands him a card. It has sparkles on it. I love sparkles, but something about Miss Isobel is just a little too sparkly for comfort. She makes me want to turn off a light somewhere.

When we get to Dad's door, Mewkiss Membrane greets me by rubbing against my leg. Mewkiss Membrane is a great name for a cat. As soon as I heard it, I knew I was going to like Steve Marshall and his kids. They are the ones who own the house where Dad rents his apartment. They live upstairs, and normally Mewkiss does too.

"What's he doing down here?" I ask.

"Steve and the kids are gone for the weekend," Dad says. "I'm taking care of Mewkiss until they get back."

Mom has allergies, which is why we

never had a pet at home. When Dad moved out, I had thought maybe I could finally have a dog at his place. But he works such long hours during the week he says it wouldn't be fair to a dog. So I have remained petless.

At least I have Gorilla.

I like Mewkiss, but he is not my ideal pet . . . . . he coughs up too many hair balls. Also, he likes leaving dead mice in the bathroom as presents for his people. I know this because one night I stayed upstairs with the Marshall kids. When I got up in the morning to go to the bathroom, I stepped on one of Mewkiss's "presents."

I, Amber Brown, can tell you from personal experience that a dead mouse under your bare foot is not the best way to start your day.

Also, waking up the other people in the house because you are screaming does not make them happy.

According to Steve, dead mice are a cat's way of saying it cares about you. That may be true, but I still think it's disgusting.

What is not disgusting is that every Friday night, Dad and I order Chinese food. Dad and I are both great at cooking with our fingertips. That is, we can grab the phone and minutes later have a delicious meal on the way to our door.

When the food comes, Dad and I have a ritual. We open all the boxes and spread them out on the coffee table. We always get spring rolls, dumplings, and General Tso's chicken, which we call "The Chicken of General Tso What?" We also get one new thing we have never tried before. We can eat the food in any order, including fortune cookies first if we want.

This is way different from the way things are at home. Mom says that eating the fortune cookies first invites chaos.

And Max believes that family dinners should be family time, without other distractions. So now we never eat dinner and watch TV at the same time. I think Mom worries that we had gotten into bad habits when Dad lived at home.

When I am with Dad, things are more relaxed. I like it because it reminds me of the old days. Except, of course, that Mom is not with us.

Ever since Dad took me to New York City to see a Broadway show, we have started a new tradition. With the Chinese food we watch a movie musical. Tonight it's *Seven Brides for Seven Brothers*.

"The dancing is so amazing," I say to Dad at the end. "It makes me excited about working with Miss Isobel."

Dad grins. "I think the world would be a better place if people burst out singing and dancing more often in real life."

Then we sing "Bless Yore Beautiful Hide," one of the songs from the movie, while we dance around cleaning up the leftovers. We aren't as good as the people in the film, but it's still a lot of fun.

"Time for bed," Dad sings when we are done.

I hurry off to brush my teeth and get on my pj's. When I come back into the living room to tell Dad good night, he is at the computer.

"Look," he says. "Your dance teacher has a website. There are videos of her dancing."

We watch a few of them. Miss Isobel really is a good dancer.

"All right," Dad says after a few minutes. "Off you go."

We head for my room and Dad tucks me in and kisses me good night.

A minute later Mewkiss Membrane

hops onto the bed and cuddles up next to me. I stroke his head, and he begins to purr. It's a very nice sound.

"No mice!" I tell him sternly.

I hope he listens.

Chapter Six

I, Amber Brown, think there should be a law against making kids go to school on a perfect spring Saturday. I am sure I am right about this because Mrs. Holt told us that the Constitution of the United States forbids "cruel and unusual" punishment. I am not sure how unusual Saturday Academy is . . . . . . but it is definitely cruel.

Dad pulls up in front of the high school. It is fifty billion times bigger than my school. Well, maybe not that big. But it is so big that it is scary.

Dad pats me on my shoulder. "Do well on your tests, Amber, and someday you may be going here for real."

"Do you think that's funny?" I growl at him.

Dad blinks. "It was just a joke, honey."

I cross my arms. "There is nothing funny about me having to go to Saturday Academy!"

Dad looks like he wants to say something else but decides not to, which is probably good. Instead he gets out of the car. I climb out my side. Even though I am a little mad at him, I am glad he is going to walk me into the school. As we get close to the door, I reach out and take his hand.

A sign taped to the glass reads SATURDAY ACADEMY IS IN THE LANGUAGE LAB.

"That sign would be more useful if we knew where the Language Lab is," Dad says.

Then he opens the door for me.

It takes us ten minutes to find the right room, and the class has already started by the time we get there. Not only do I get to be the new kid, I get to be the new kid who came late.

I look around to see if there is anyone I know. I spot two fifth graders who I have never talked to, a fourth grader who goes to our church, and . . . . . I should have guessed . . . . Bobby Clifford.

Bobby. I really am at the bottom of the aquarium.

The teacher is talking but stops when we come in. He sees me, then glances down at a list on his desk. "Ah, you must be Amber Brown." He smiles. "A very colorful name. Colorful, but not an excuse for being late."

I like my colorful name. I'm not sure I like him.

He points to an empty seat. It's right beside Bobby.

Next time I'll make sure I'm here early.

"My name is Mr. Poindexter."

For some reason I think that's funny. Bobby catches my eyes. I look out the window before he can make me laugh. I don't need to get in any more trouble in my first five minutes.

Dad waves good–bye and abandons me.

Mr. Poindexter puts a math problem on the Smart Board. It's not smart, it's stupid. (The problem, not the board.) A girl named Mariella is taking a train. The train leaves Mariella's town and travels for one hour and forty-five minutes.

I start to worry about her. They don't even tell us if Mariella is old enough to take a train by herself. And what if she gets hungry? Is there a snack car?

After the first stop of ten minutes, the train travels another four hours and forty minutes. It arrives at 12:50 A.M.

"The question is," Mr. Poindexter says, "what time did Mariella's journey begin?"

Personally, I think a better question would be, "How many times did Mariella have to go to the bathroom before the train reached its destination?"

This makes me think of a song Aunt Pam taught me:

Passengers will please refrain
From flushing toilets
While the train
Is standing in the station.
I love you.

I think she just added the "I love you" to go with the melody.

Mr. Poindexter says, "Amber, how would you find the solution?"

This is difficult to answer since I had gotten so distracted that I forgot what the actual problem was.

While I am trying to remember, Bobby

says, "Why did Mariella's parents let her take a train that got in at 12:50 A.M. anyway? That doesn't sound very safe to me."

I look at him. I am not sure if he is being a wise guy or if he is trying to help me out.

Mr. Poindexter sighs and demonstrates how to solve the problem . . . . . which turns out to be "What time did the train leave the station?"

Writing on the Smart Board, he says, "You just add together the two travel times and the rest time. Subtract the total . . . . . six hours and thirty-five minutes . . . from the time she arrived, 12:50 A.M. Bingo! We find that Mariella left at 6:15 P.M."

The girl in front of me says, "But that's so simple!"

Mr. Poindexter smiles. "Exactly! For many of these problems, the math is easy.

The trick is not to get lost in the extra words."

Uh-oh. That was exactly what happened to me. I got lost in the words. Well, the words and my own thoughts.

Maybe I do have a focus problem!

"Just look for what the real question is," Mr. Poindexter says. "And remember, these tests are multiple choice, so you will always have the right answer in front of you."

Then he passes out work sheets with ten problems and tells us we have thirty minutes to solve them.

The problems are all about trains, planes, and automobiles.

After I read them, I feel like I need training wheels. I am definitely lost in the words.

I glance over at Bobby. I've seen him look silly, mad, goofy, mean, and weird.

But until today I didn't realize he had a sad face. I would feel sorry for him, but he is also driving me crazy. He can't sit still. He squirms in his chair. He drums his fingers on the desk. He drops his pencil three times. In between he gets up to sharpen it. The last time he also manages to poke me in the arm on his way back to his desk.

Mr. Poindexter yells at him to sit down.

Bobby not only sits down, he puts his head down.

Mr. Poindexter says, "Time's up! Everyone pass your paper to the person in front of you. People in the front row, take your paper to the last person in the row."

This makes me think of the hoedown Dad and I saw in *Seven Brides for Seven Brothers* last night. If only there was music, this would be a lot more fun. Right now it's no fun at all.

Mr. Poindexter puts the answers on the Smart Board. The person I am grading got eight out of ten. I got three. I wonder how many Bobby got. I don't think it was very many because he has put his head down on his desk again. I'm not sure, but I think he might be crying.

I know how he feels.

Chapter Seven

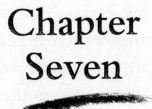

"How was it?" Dad asks.

"Next week can I stay home and stick a fork in my eye?" I answer. "It might be more fun."

"That bad, huh? Well, cheer up. Let's get some lunch. Then I've got something special planned for this afternoon."

"What is it?"

Dad smiles. "It's a surprise."

"Tell me!"

"If I tell you, it won't be a surprise."

I roll my eyes at him, but I don't bug him to tell me more. I like surprises . . . . .

as long as they are good ones. And Dad is good at surprises. His last one was our trip to the Broadway musical. It was one of the best things that we've ever done together.

After lunch we don't go to Broadway. Instead we drive to the next town over. Dad turns into a little mall and parks in front of a store called You've Got Nail!

"Are you getting me sparkly toenails?" I squeal.

Dad laughs. "No. Look at the next sign."

I do. It says MOVE AND GROOVE DANCE STUDIO.

Dad smiles. "I e-mailed Isobel last night and she invited us to visit her studio. I'm thinking of taking dance lessons myself."

"Really?"

Dad laughs. "Don't sound so surprised. I need to get out of my comfort zone."

"Who says?"

Dad looks down and mumbles, "Lots of people."

I have a feeling that by "lots of people" he really means one person . . . . . his counselor. Dad told me he's seeing her for "dad lessons" and I know he is trying to be a better dad. But I've figured out that he probably talks to her about other things too.

"Come on," he says. "Let's get a move on."

I am not sure how I feel about this. It's like Dad is moving into my territory. Besides, I did dance at school yesterday. Then I went to school this morning. Now we're back at another school-type thing this afternoon. That's enough school!

On the other hand, the dancing was fun.

On the other other hand . . . . . . which makes three in all, which makes me feel like an alien . . . . part of me just wants to go back to Dad's and do nothing for a while.

While I am thinking all of this, Dad

has made it halfway to the door. I scurry to catch up with him.

We step into a small room. It has life-size pictures of Isobel dancing. She is dressed in gowns that have more sparkles than even I have ever dreamed of. In a glass case are several shiny trophies that have dancing couples on top.

Miss Isobel comes out to greet us. "I'm so glad to see you again, Topaz."

"It's Amber," Dad quickly says. "Amber Brown. She's named for the color."

Miss Isobel smiles. "Topaz is a color too, no? And they are both jewels. A girl can't have enough jewels."

I never thought I would have nothing to say about my name, but Miss Isobel has me stumped.

"Come," she says. "Come see the studio."

We follow her into a large room. It has a shiny wooden floor, and one whole wall is covered with mirrors.

Miss Isobel looks at Dad. "Did you bring your dance shoes?"

He glances down at his sneakers. "Uh, dance shoes?"

Miss Isobel rolls her eyes. "Sneakers are not good for the dance! They squeak. It is appalling. You need leather soles for the turns." She sighs. "For today, you can dance in your socks."

She waves Dad to the bench.

I go with him. "This is my surprise?" I say as he unlaces his sneakers. "I get to watch you have a lesson?"

Dad looks a little desperate. "Isobel said if I brought you, she'd have a nice surprise for you too."

"Ruby," Miss Isobel calls.

I don't even bother to correct her. I am beginning to wonder if she is doing this on purpose. Does she think it's funny? Is this a joke where she comes from?

"I asked Ramón to come in today," she

says. "He is one of my students. He is also the teenage New Jersey champion in Latin dance. I am going to bring him to your school later in the program, but I think it will be nice for you to meet him now."

Ramón comes in through a door in the back wall. He is wearing a black Move and Groove T-shirt, black pants, and shiny black shoes. He smiles at me.

If Brandi and Kelly could see me, I know they would be jealous. Ramón is as cute as the boys on the posters that decorate Brandi's bedroom.

I wonder if I can get a poster of him for my new room.

"We will begin with the samba," Miss Isobel says. "It is a wonderful dance from Brazil, very beautiful. And it is not one that we will be doing at school, Jade."

"It's Amber," I mutter.

Miss Isobel waves her hand. Her fingernails are sparkly. I wonder if she gets them done at You've Got Nail!

Ramón smiles at me again and says, "I like the name Amber."

I feel myself start to blush.

Isobel gestures for Ramón to join her in

the center of the room. "Now, come close and watch," she says to Dad and me. "Ramón and I will demonstrate. We will do the steps without music first, very slowly. It starts with the samba bounce."

Their feet stay in place, but their hips begin to move.

"The hip movement is done on the half beat," Miss Isobel says.

Dad looks scared. "I have no idea what she's talking about," he whispers.

Ramón and Isobel begin to dance. It is as if a different species has entered the room. They are moving in a way that doesn't seem possible, but it is beautiful. Then they break apart.

"Now you will try it with us," Miss Isobel says. "Don't worry, we start very slowly."

Isobel goes to Dad. Ramón takes my hand.

"Just follow me, Amber. When I step forward, you go backward with your left leg."

I look down.

"No!" Ramón says. "Look at me, not your feet."

I do. Ramón is much better looking than my feet. He's got the longest eyelashes I have ever seen.

Miss Isobel counts the beats very slowly. As she does, I try to imitate Ramón's moves. When he moves forward, my left foot goes back. It's like magic. My feet are doing what they're supposed to without my thinking about it.

"Good," Ramón says. "Now add the hips."

"Not me," I say.

"It's easy, Periwinkle." He winks at me. "Just move from the knees."

I giggle, but I think my hips are moving.

I look over at Dad and Miss Isobel. He is biting the tip of his tongue, a sure sign that he is concentrating. He looks serious, but happy too.

We try the dance with music. After several times I am not stepping on Ramón's feet. I am actually feeling the music . . . . . . moving to it . . . . and turning when Ramón signals me. I'm dancing!

When the session ends, Miss Isobel curtsies to Dad. I remember what she taught us and I curtsy to Ramón. He bows and smiles at me.

I look at Dad. He has not bowed. I clear my throat. Then I clear it again. He looks at me and I nod my head toward Miss

Isobel. Dad's eyes get wide. Then he turns to Miss Isobel and bows.

Sometimes I worry about him.

As we get in the car, Dad turns to me. "That was fun, wasn't it?"

I smile at him and say, "Yep."

He sighs. "I've got to take you home now, remember."

"It's not really fair," I tell him. "I'd rather spend the whole weekend with you."

"I know, but your mom said that you all have a lot to do to finish getting ready for the move. Once it's over, you and I will get to spend some extra days together."

I pout.

Dad pats my hand. "Careful, Amber, your face will freeze that way."

"You've been telling me that since I was two and it hasn't happened yet."

He laughs. "There's always a first time," he warns.

We pull up to my house. Dad has been

quiet for most of the drive. When I turn to kiss him good-bye, he looks sad.

I put my hand on his arm. "What's wrong, Dad?"

"This is the last time I'll ever drop you off at this house." He sighs. "This is where I brought you home after you were born. It's where I watched you grow up. I know I don't live here anymore, but it was my home for a long time, and as long as you and your mom were here, I felt like I hadn't lost it completely. But now it will be gone for good."

Suddenly I feel like crying.

We sit side by side and stare at the house. I start to sniffle.

Dad looks at me, then smiles and says, "Don't cry, Topaz."

This makes me laugh a little, even though I am still crying. I think it is very strange that people can laugh and cry at the same time.

"Come on," he says. "I'll walk you to the door."

"Do you want to come in?" I ask him.

I'm not sure if I want him to or not, but I feel like I should ask.

Dad shakes his head. "I don't think that's a good idea."

He gives me a hug, then turns and walks back to his car.

Chapter
Eight

I, Amber Brown, used to live in a house.
I went away for a night and a day and
while I was gone, Mom and Max turned
the place into a disaster zone.

They have filled our home with boxes.
There are boxes everywhere. Boxes for
the books . . . . . boxes for the dishes . . . . .
boxes for the glasses . . . . . boxes for the
towels. I know what they are for because
Max has labeled each one with a Magic
Marker.

He has also numbered them.

Walking between all the boxes makes me feel like a mouse in a maze.

"Look how much we've done," Max says proudly. "We finished the kitchen and made a good start on the living room."

I look into what used to be the living room. There are no pictures on the walls, no books on the shelves, no knickknacks on the end tables. Mom is kneeling on the floor with a box labeled SARAH'S SEASHELLS.

I point to the label. "Bet you can't say that three times fast."

"Careful," Mom says. "I lost my sense of humor when we hit box number fifty."

"But we've made such progress!" Max exclaims.

Mom scowls at him.

"I think I'll go fill the tape gun," he says.

I kneel next to Mom and start wrapping a seashell.

"Did you have a good time with your dad?" she asks.

I nod.

"You don't seem very happy."

I look around the room at all the boxes. "I don't want to move. I love this house. And it doesn't help any that Max is so cheerful about leaving."

"Amber, we've been over this a dozen times. Max, you, and I need a house that is ours, that is fresh."

"You and Max want a house that is fresh. I was perfectly happy with this one. And it's not stale."

Mom's face gets stern. "The movers are coming in five days, and you just need to accept it."

I put down the seashell I was wrapping. "Fine."

I do not mean that, of course. I mean just the opposite. I wonder if anyone has ever said "fine" and meant it.

I get to my feet and head for the stairs.

"Amber," Mom calls.

I don't answer, and I don't think she really expects me to.

I go to my room. I love my room. It has three yellow walls. The fourth wall has dancing ballerina wallpaper. Only these ballerinas are hippos, ducks, elephants, rhinos, and rabbits. I know it's kind of babyish, and I wanted to change it just a few months ago. But now that I have to leave it behind, I know I'm going to miss it. I bet the new owners will paint over it. That makes me mad just to think about.

The only thing I don't like about my room is that stupid box labeled AMBER'S TOYS TO DONATE. It is still sitting there. And it is still empty.

I hear a knock on the door frame. It's Max. He is carrying the tape gun. "Can I come in?"

I shrug. "Sure."

"I wanted to get to work on your room

while you were gone, Amber, but your mom told me I had to wait for you."

"Mom was right."

Max frowns. "It's just that I'm worried your room won't be ready in time for the movers."

Although he stayed calm through the wedding, since Max has been living with us, I've learned that "I'm worried" are two of his favorite words.

And I thought Mom was the worrywart.

Now I've got two worrywarts to deal with.

Which is one more thing for me to worry about.

I hope worrying doesn't really cause warts. It was one thing to have chicken pox. I don't want a batch of worry warts popping out all over my face.

While I am worrying about warts, Max sits down on the edge of my bed. He looks around.

"I know you love this room," he says, as if he could read my mind. "But I promise we'll work to make your new room even better. Don't forget, you're going to have your own bathroom. That will be a big improvement, won't it?"

"Just because something is better doesn't mean I want to trade in the old thing that I love to get it," I say.

Max nods. "I understand that. But Amber, can you try to understand that I can't really live here in this house that your mom shared with your dad for so long? I know I might seem a little over-the-top about this move, but I've always lived in apartments and I've never had a house of my own. Having a new home for our new family just feels right to me."

"And leaving this house feels wrong to me!"

"You've known we were going to be doing this for a long time now, Amber."

"Well, it's different now that it's happening!" As I say that, I realize it is true.

Max shakes his head. "As my mother used to say, the train has left the station."

"What's that supposed to mean?"

"It means everything is in motion and there's no turning back. This move is going to happen whether you want it to or not. So the only question now is, how hard are you going to make things for yourself?"

He points to my shelves, which are full of games, crafts, toys, glitter, and books. "You haven't even begun to sort through this stuff. Let's do it now. What do you want to throw out?"

I know I can't say, "You!" but that's the first thing that I think. The next thing I think is that after I throw him out, I want to take the tape gun and tape my door shut so that nobody can get in.

"I'll do it later," I say to him.

"It's never going to get done if you don't get started! Let's do it now."

"I'll do it later," I say again.

"No, we need to start now!"

I open my mouth, and what comes out surprises me. "You're not my father!"

Max's eyes get wide and his face turns red. But he doesn't say anything. He just gets up and leaves my room.

I feel sick. I was kind of mean to Max when Mom first started to date him, but after a while I got to like him, and then I even came to love him. We have never been really mad at each other before, but right now I don't like him at all.

It scares me how sad that makes me.

I pick up Gorilla. "Too bad you aren't real. Then you could help me pack." I look around my room. "I could use an army of gorillas."

Then I get a brilliant idea. I may not have a gorilla army, but I've got a girl army.

I call Brandi. She can tell from my voice that I'm upset. "What's wrong?" she asks.

"I just had my first big fight with Max."

"About what?"

"This stupid packing for this stupid move. I haven't even started and Max is getting nervous. The movers aren't even coming until Thursday."

"Thursday? Yikes! You do need help, Amber. Lucky for you, you have friends."

She bursts into song. "That's what friends are for!"

I giggle.

"Seriously, I'll get Kelly and we'll come over tomorrow. It'll be fun. And don't worry about Max . . . . . just tell him you're sorry and the troops are coming to the rescue. We'll get this done."

Just talking to her makes me feel better. I take a minute to calm down, then go to look for Max.

He hasn't gone very far . . . . he's sitting at the top of the stairs kind of looking at nothing.

I sit beside him and say, "I'm sorry."

He doesn't say anything.

"You were right," I say, trying again. "I do need help. Brandi and Kelly are coming tomorrow and we'll get my room done."

"Fine," he says.

I know what that means.

Then he takes a deep breath. "Listen, Amber, I'm not trying to replace your dad. But I'm in your life and sometimes I have to be the grown-up. We're going to have fights sometimes. I'm glad you said you're sorry. And I'm sorry if I was pushing too hard, but I really am worried. I'm glad Brandi and Kelly are coming tomorrow."

He takes the tape gun and goes downstairs to help Mom.

"Max!" I call. "We'll need your help labeling the boxes."

He turns and smiles. "I'm on it!"

Chapter Nine

"Ta-da! Help has arrived!"

That's Brandi. She's standing in my doorway.

"And not a minute too soon from the looks of things. Amber, haven't you done any packing at all?"

That's Kelly. She is looking over Brandi's shoulder into my room.

I shrug, feeling a little embarrassed. "I kept waiting for the packing fairy, but she never showed up."

"Well, the first thing we need is more boxes," Brandi says.

"No problem there. Didn't you see the stacks piled right outside my door waiting to be made up? We'll have to get Max's tape gun, though."

"Not necessary," Kelly says. She reaches into her backpack and pulls out a tape gun. "We still had this around from our last move. I figured it would come in handy."

It turns out it's fun to make boxes. I like seeing things that are flat turn into things that aren't flat. And the tape, which is two inches wide, makes a cool ripping sound as it comes off the big roll.

"Turn it over," Brandi says when I get the first box ready for taping. "That's the top. You don't want to tape that up yet."

I look at her. "What difference does it make which end is the top and which is the bottom? It's a box."

"The top has places for you to write what's inside," Kelly explains. "See, there's a line for your name, another line for what's in it. That way the movers will put the boxes in your room, which is where you want them, and you'll know which boxes you want to unpack first."

She sounds a lot like Max now. I decide not to mention that.

Kelly is in her take-charge mode. "You need two boxes and a garbage bag going all the time. One box is for things to keep, one is for things to donate, and the garbage bag is for stuff too junky to give away. We've moved three times, and the important thing is not to take too much with you. In our family we have one rule for moving: Throw out, throw out, throw out."

"I feel more like throwing up," I say. "I don't want to throw anything away. I love my stuff."

Brandi laughs. "So do those crazy people you see on TV who can't walk through their houses because they've got so much junk. You don't want to end up like them, Amber. Most of this stuff you'll never miss."

"That's what Justin said. But I don't get it. I'm moving into a bigger house. Why do I have to get rid of anything? I'll have room for all my stuff."

Kelly says, "What you need is room for new stuff. Look, Amber, some of the things you've got around here are pretty babyish."

"They are not."

Brandi laughs again. "Really? What about this?" She goes to my shelf and picks up a plastic duck on wheels that quacks when you pull it behind you.

I laugh. "You're quacking me up. Okay, that is pretty babyish. But it was my favorite toy when I was two."

This causes Kelly to start singing "My Favorite Things." Brandi and I join in.

We dance around the room. As we do, I pick up some of my favorite things . . . . the blue plastic mermaid that plays music when you press the jewel in her belly, the pig-taking-a-bubble-bath bank that is also an alarm clock, and the plastic reindeer that poops miniature jelly beans. I hand each one to Brandi, who wraps it and puts it in the To Keep box.

The second time we get to the line "These are a few of my favorite things," Kelly stops singing and says, "Did you notice that the song says a FEW of my favorite things, Amber? Not every single thing I ever owned in my entire life?"

I don't think it is fair to use a song against me, but I have to admit that I understand her point.

Brandi says, "Your new room should be about Amber now, not about baby Amber."

She's making sense. I go to a bottom shelf filled with toys that I haven't looked at for at least a year. Except for my "pass-port" from Mr. Cohen's third-grade class, I throw everything else into the To Donate box. It makes me happy to think of some little kid having fun with these toys. It makes me happy for the toys too since I personally believe that toys want to be played with.

I probably should have done this sooner.

When I am finished with the shelf, the box is full. While Kelly shoves it out of the way, Brandi brings me another To Donate box.

I fill that one too. I realize Justin, Kelly, and Brandi were right . . . . . . it is mostly baby stuff. In fact, some of it is embarrass-ing, like the stuffed cat that only has three legs because I chewed the fourth one off when I was teething.

We start on my bookshelves. This is harder because I love my books, even the ones I had when I was very little. It also goes more slowly because Brandi and Kelly and I talk about a lot of the books, especially the ones we've all read. Finally I decide to keep them all.

"I want these in case I ever have kids of my own," I say.

Mom comes in and looks at what we've done so far. "Wow," she says. "I think you girls have earned a pizza break."

"And here it is," Max says, walking in with a pizza box and a big bottle of soda.

We have a pizza-nic on my bed.

It is a nice break from packing. It is also a good chance for some girl talk.

"So what's it like having to dance with Fredrich?" Kelly asks.

Brandi sighs. "He's really good. I just wish everyone in class didn't still think of him as Mr. Booger Paws. It's kind of embarrassing."

"I think Fredrich is nice," I say.

I didn't used to think that. I didn't used

to think about Fredrich much at all, except for the fact that he was a nose picker. But when we had Mom and Max's wedding at the camp Fredrich's family owns, I got to know him a little better. Now I am kind of embarrassed about how I used to treat him.

"It's weird how you don't know who would be a good dancer," Kelly says. "I noticed Bobby isn't half bad either."

"And I'm not half good," I say.

Kelly and Brandi laugh a little too hard at that.

"How is Gregory?" Brandi asks. Gregory is who Kelly got paired with.

Kelly makes a face. "He's not bad, except every time he makes a mistake he says 'sorry' in burp talk!"

Brandi laughs. "It's too bad we need boys for dancing. It would be so much easier without them."

I think of Ramón and how easy he

made the dancing when I was with him. I decide not to mention that.

"Okay, we'd better get started again," Kelly says. "We still have to tackle your closet. That's going to be a biggie."

My closet is scary. Soon my bed is covered with clothes. Brandi and Kelly have very strong opinions on what to keep. Luckily we agree that I don't need the leggings from second grade that have daisies on them. In fact, we get rid of a lot of the leggings.

I tell Brandi and Kelly that they are pulling my leggings.

They groan, but laugh.

Then Brandi says, "Okay, the rule is if you haven't worn something since third grade, it has to go."

I agree, though I do insist on keeping the I Love London T-shirt that I got from my trip with Aunt Pam.

As we keep going, the Donate pile gets bigger than the Take It with Me pile.

I find the daisy dress that went with the leggings. It still almost fits. I hold it up. "I think I'll keep this."

Brandi shakes her head.

"I'm starting a Maybe pile," I say.

Kelly looks alarmed.

"I promise to keep it small," I tell her.

Soon we can see the floor of my closet. I don't remember the last time I saw my closet floor.

I haul out my pink glitter bowling ball. Max gave it to me. It has my name engraved on it. It goes in the To Keep box.

"Bulletin! Bulletin! Bulletin!" shouts Brandi. She's on all fours halfway in my closet. "Amber Brown has a strange alien artifact in a shoe box in her closet."

She backs out, and I see that she is holding the box that has the chewing gum ball. "Amber, what in the world is this?"

"Let me see," Kelly says.

"Give it to me," I say. "It's private."

I wrap my arms around the box.

"What is it?" Brandi asks again.

"Something Justin and I made. I keep it because it helps me remember him."

Kelly laughs. "Wouldn't a picture be better?"

"You guys don't understand. Justin lived next door and he was my best friend. He was in and out of this house almost every day. Now I'll never live in a house where he was my neighbor. And I will never, ever live in a house where Mom and Dad and I were together."

Brandi and Kelly are quiet for a moment. Then Brandi goes over to the bed and picks up the daisy dress. "Maybe you should keep this one after all," she says.

We go back to work.

Chapter Ten

I, Amber Brown, am discombobulated. So is my house. Boxes, boxes everywhere and not a place to think . . . . . or even sit down. That's because the movers are coming this morning.

Personally, I think "The movers are coming, the movers are coming!" is an even more frightening sentence than "The Martians are coming, the Martians are coming!"

Mom puts a paper plate in front of me. "Peanut butter for breakfast," she says.

It's my favorite . . . . . . an English muffin decorated with M&M's to make a smiley face.

I am impressed that she somehow managed to keep the toaster from landing in one of Max's boxes. I think about moving the M&M's to make a frowny face, but decide it is a bad idea.

Max is too nervous to eat breakfast. He keeps going to the front door to see if the moving van has showed up yet.

"They were supposed to be here by eight," he says.

"Relax," Mom tells him. "They'll be here."

Max gives me a smile. It's his "I'm pretending not to be worried" smile.

I've started making a list of Max's worried faces. I wonder if I can do them in M&M's. I wonder if I made him one on an English muffin if he would eat it.

Mom jangles her keys and says, "All right, Amber, I'll drive you to school now."

Max smiles a real smile. "Just think, Amber, after school you won't be coming here, you'll go straight to our new house!"

I do think about this. It is not a happy thought.

I look around. It is the last time I will be leaving for school from this house. My house. Except it doesn't look like my house anymore, it looks like a place for boxes.

"Amber, come on," Mom says impatiently. "We've got to get going."

"Not yet," I say. I run up to my room. Like the rest of the house, it is filled with boxes. The shelves are empty. My closet is empty.

I kiss the door frame. "Good-bye, room," I whisper. "I will miss you."

Trying not to cry, I run back down the stairs. I rush past Max without kissing him good-bye and out to Mom's car.

I get in my side. Mom gets in the driver's side. She puts on her sunglasses. I can't see her eyes.

When we get to school, she gives me a kiss. "Wish me luck," she says.

I get out of the car. I don't wish her luck. She doesn't notice.

I go to the cafeteria, which is where the kids who get to school early are supposed to wait until first bell. I sit by myself. A few minutes later Mrs. Holt spots me as she is walking by.

She comes in and says, "It's moving day, isn't it, Amber? I'm glad you're not moving far away. I would hate to lose you."

I am feeling lost anyway, but I don't say that. I know it would be stupid to say that I feel like I am homeless when so many people really are homeless. But I really don't feel like I have a home right now.

"I could use some help," Mrs. Holt says. "Why don't you come with me?"

I am glad to leave the cafeteria.

When we get to our classroom, Mrs. Holt says, "Would you like to help me finish this new bulletin board, Amber?"

Big red letters at the top of the bulletin

board say OUR CLASS HAS THE RIGHT
MOVES.

"It's a surprise for Miss Isobel," she tells
me. "It was Mr. Robinson's idea. He went
to her website and found all these great
pictures from when she was a champion
dancer."

I begin to think my father and Mr.
Robinson have a lot in common.

Mrs. Holt asks me to help her decide
how to place the pictures. We take turns
stapling them to the bulletin board.

"You have a very artistic eye, Amber,"
she says.

I can't help myself. I smile. It's my first
smile of the day.

I have never had a day go so slow and
so fast at the same time. Part of me wants
school to be over so I can get to the new
house. Part of me wants the school day to
never end.

It does.

I was expecting Mom to pick me up, but it is Max instead.

"What are you doing here?" I ask. I realize that sounds rude, so I quickly add, "I mean, I was expecting Mom is all."

Max gives me a half smile. "Your mother said I should come get you because I was driving the movers nuts telling them where to put each box and in what order."

"Are they still unloading?" I ask him.

He nods. "I think they're moving in." He looks at my face. "That's a joke."

"I got it. I'm glad you can still make jokes."

Max shrugs. "It's what I do when things get tense."

I look at him. "I thought you were all excited about this."

"I am! But that doesn't mean it's not hard . . . . . and tiring! Remember, I went through it just a little while ago when I moved in with your mom and you. And this is a much bigger move." He makes a face. "I know I've been a little bit of a pain about this."

"You have," I say.

"You didn't have to agree so quickly!" He smiles at me.

The drive home is very strange since we are traveling on streets that I've never seen before.

The houses in our new neighborhood all look kind of alike . . . . all brand-new . . . . . . even the ones like Kelly's that have people living in them. The only way I can tell which one is ours is by the huge moving van parked in front of it.

We go inside and I discover there is one way in which the new house is just like the house we left behind. There are boxes everywhere!

My mother is wearing a scarf over her hair and has a smudge of dirt on her nose. "Welcome home," she says. "Well, almost home. It will feel more like home in a while."

Two big men come past her. They are carrying a couch. It is not our couch, so it

must be the one that belonged to Max. It is clean and new looking.

I wonder how long it will stay that way. Which makes me wonder if Max really knows what it is going to be like to have a kid in the house.

Chapter
Eleven

I, Amber Brown, am standing outside our old house. Mom is beside me. We went out to pick up Chinese food while Max stayed home to open boxes. But we have made a detour to do one last thing.

Mom is holding a bottle of red wine and an envelope. I am also holding an envelope, only mine has glitter and stars. Both envelopes say the same thing on the outside . . . . . WELCOME TO YOUR NEW HOME.

We go inside. It feels strange and empty.

We walk into the kitchen. No table . . . .
no chairs . . . . . the only place to put anything is on the counter. Mom sets down
the bottle of wine. She leans her envelope
against it, then picks it up again and says,
"Would you like to hear what I wrote?"

I nod.

Mom opens her envelope and takes out
the letter.

Welcome to your new home. I've included a list of plumbers, electricians, our favorite pizza place, the best place for Chinese takeout, and a fun bowling alley. I hope you will find it useful.

Even more, I hope you will be as happy here as I have been. This house has seen a lot of joy and, of course, some sorrow. I hope your time here will be one of much joy and little sorrow.

May you love this place as much as I did.

Sarah Turner

Mom folds the letter back up.

"I thought you weren't happy here," I say.

"Not true. This house has a lot of wonderful memories."

"Even with Dad?" I ask, thinking of the horrible year when they were deciding if they could stay together and then told me that they couldn't.

"Yes, especially with him," Mom says. "This is where we brought you home. This is where we watched you grow up."

"That's what Dad said. Do you want to hear what I wrote?"

"I'd love to, if you don't mind."

Dear New Owners—

I hope you like glitter because I wrote this with my glitter pen. I use glitter a lot . . . . . you might find a little bit of it here and there, especially in my room. It is at the top of the stairs.

I love my room and I got to decorate it myself. I don't know who will be living there now, but I want them to have fun.

This house has had a lot of fun and some sad times too.

I look at Mom. "We wrote almost the same thing."

"It's the truth," she says.

I smile. "Now let me read the rest of this."

I, Amber Brown, have loved all of this house . . . . . and I hope you will too. Here is a joke I wrote just to welcome you:

"Knock knock."

"Who's there?"

"Hope."

"Hope who?"

"Hope you will be happy in your new home!"

Your friend who has never met you,
                    Amber Brown

Chapter Twelve

Miss Isobel flings open the classroom door. She looks at the wall and cries, "The bulletin board! It is lovely!"

She has come to pick us up for Friday afternoon dancing, but the bulletin board has distracted her.

Mrs. Holt smiles and says, "Amber helped design it."

"Then we must have our picture taken in front of it!" exclaims Miss Isobel. She places me next to her.

I wait for her to mangle my name. She

doesn't. She simply whispers, "Stand sideways. That's the way to take a good photo."

We angle toward each other. Mrs. Holt takes our picture.

Some of the kids are snickering, and I start to feel embarrassed. On the other hand, I am happy she liked the bulletin board. And it's kind of neat learning that trick for photos.

Sometimes I think that everything that happens in my life has at least two emotions attached to it.

It can be very confusing to be me.

At the dance lesson we learn the T-A-N-G-O.

Miss Isobel claps. This is not to applaud, it is her way of getting our attention. "Now lift your left hands above your heads," she orders. "Curve your arms when you make the turn. They should look like a scorpion's tail. Press your forearms together like peanut butter and jelly. Look at Fredrich and Brandi . . . . . they are doing it just right."

"I love peanut butter," Bobby says. He licks his arm, then presses it against mine. I am disgusted. But then when we actually do this part of the dance, he is really good at it. I am not. In fact, I am so not good at it that I am making him look bad too.

"Come on, Amber. Pay attention!"

Having Bobby Clifford tell you to pay attention is like having a kindergartener tell you to grow up.

"I'll count it out for us," he says. "It will be easier that way."

Mrs. Holt is standing nearby. She touches Bobby's shoulder. "I am proud of you. Miss Isobel said that you students would learn kindness from dance . . . . to actually see it . . . ."

Bobby blushes, and I decide not to tell Mrs. Holt that he was more frustrated than kind.

When Mrs. Holt has moved away, Bobby says, "Look, Amber, I really want to win this. It's a contest, remember?"

I realize that as far as I know, Bobby has never won anything before.

I try harder, and this time when we do the scorpion, I don't trip on my feet.

At the end of the lesson I go to get my backpack. As I pick it up, Mrs. Holt says,

"Amber, can I have a minute with you, please?"

I want to say, "No! School is over for the week!" but I know that would not be smart. So instead I say, "My dad is waiting for me."

"Yes, I know. I've spoken to him already. He said he would be happy to wait a bit longer." She smiles and adds, "I think he wanted to help Miss Isobel pack up."

I sigh and follow Mrs. Holt back to our room. When I was messing up the dance, I felt like I had two left feet. Now I feel like I have a concrete block tied to each foot.

Mrs. Holt motions for me to sit next to her desk. She sits and faces me. Then she says four of my least favorite words in the world. . . . . . "Amber, I'm still worried."

I get a knot in my stomach. Hearing those words from Mrs. Holt is scary. And

I don't mean Halloween scary. I mean "life as I know it is about to end" scary.

"Mr. Poindexter has been in touch with me. Your scores on the practice tests at Saturday Academy are still in the danger zone. He says that particularly in the math problems, you get lost in the words. I know you're smart, Amber, but you're just not using your brainpower. If you don't pull your scores up for the real test in two weeks, I don't want to think of the consequences."

I want to pretend I don't know what she means . . . . . . but my stomach is telling me that I do know . . . . . . summer school instead of summer camp.

"What should I do?" I ask her. I am trying not to cry.

She answers with one word: "Focus."

I am truly sick of hearing that. "Everybody keeps telling me that," I say. "But no one tells me how!"

Mrs. Holt makes her thinking face. Finally she says, "There's no easy answer for that. But try this. . . . . Order yourself to think of one thing at a time, one problem at a time. Don't let your mind move so fast. It's a wonderful mind, Amber, but it ties you in knots sometimes. Tomorrow when you're at Saturday Academy, pay attention to how you pay attention."

"What's that supposed to mean?"

"Think of it this way. Each time you're trying to answer one of the test questions, it's like following a path through the woods. If you stick to the path, you'll get to the destination. If you go off the path to smell the flowers or chase a rabbit, you'll get lost and not find your way back. Just stick to the path."

"But people always say you should stop to smell the roses," I say.

Mrs. Holt laughs. "That's good advice for life, but not for while you're taking a test! Now scoot. I want to get home, and your dad is waiting."

I start to scoot. But at the door I stop and turn back. "Thank you," I say. "I'll try to stick to the path."

She nods and smiles, then points and says, "Right now the path leads to your dad's car."

I resume scooting. But when I get to the parking lot, I find something I wasn't expecting.

Chapter Thirteen

Dad and Miss Isobel are leaning against the Hot Tamale. Dad is laughing at something Miss Isobel has just said. He looks happier than I've seen him in a long time.

Miss Isobel smiles when she sees me. "Ah, there you are, Amethyst! I was just telling your father about that wonderful bulletin board."

"Isobel is coming home with us," Dad says happily. "She's offered to cook dinner tonight."

He's grinning at me as if this is good

news. And it is, kind of. But it's also confusing. I like Miss Isobel, and it's fun to be with her. But this was supposed to be my time with Dad.

Is he dating her?

Is she his girlfriend?

And why didn't he think to ask me before he invited her to join us for our Friday movie night?

Miss Isobel is shaking her head. "Your father tried to cook for me earlier this week. It was very sad. Tonight, I will cook. You can help if you like. Cooking is like dancing in the kitchen."

Dad says, "We've rented *Singin' in the Rain*. It's Isobel's favorite movie too."

Miss Isobel steps away from the Hot Tamale. "I will follow you home," she says. Then she climbs into her VW.

Dad and I get into the Hot Tamale.

I cross my arms over my chest.

"So, is there something I need to know? You cooked for Miss Isobel this week? And she's cooking for us tonight? And sharing our movie with us? And you never bothered to ask me what I thought about it?"

Dad blushes a little. "I suppose I should have warned you. But with the move going on this week, I didn't think it was a good idea to call." He smiles. "I was actually trying to be sensitive. You don't mind that I'm seeing Isobel, do you? I thought you liked her."

"I do like her! But this is supposed to be our night together."

"But we will be together. When Isobel heard about our movie musical night, she was so excited. Just think, we'll be watching with a real dancer."

I do think, and I think it sounds like fun. But I also think my father should have let me know before he invited Miss Isobel to join us.

I also think I have too much to think about.

When we get to the house, Miss Isobel takes a machine out of her car. "This is a food processor," she tells me. "We'll need it tonight. Your father is very nice, Aquamarine, but his kitchen . . . . oh, it is such a man kitchen. Sadly underdeveloped."

When we get inside, she heads straight for the kitchen. I notice that she seems to know her way around. My father follows her, but she turns him and pushes on his shoulders. "Go do something with the wine," she says. "Watch one of those sports things. In here, tonight, it shall be the ladies."

She sets the pot on the stove. "We are going to make pesto," she tells me. "It's so easy. Presto pesto! Fresh basil, pine nuts, a

little olive oil, and some garlic . . . . you will like. It's bright green, like an emerald."

"That's one name you haven't called me yet," I tell her.

She winks at me. "Lucky for us there are so many jewels."

Isobel and I actually have fun making dinner.

"It's time to eat and watch the movie," she tells me when we are done. "I know you have your Friday night tradition of eating in front of the TV. Of this I do not normally approve, but tradition is tradition, and this is your home."

We carry the bowls into the living room and set them on the coffee table. Dad has three wineglasses out. He pours wine into two of them. "Be right back," he says, and disappears into the kitchen. He comes out with a can of cream soda and pours some into the third glass for me. We clink glasses, then settle on the couch. Dad starts the movie. He is sitting in the center of the couch, with me on one side and Miss Isobel on the other.

I love, love, love the movie.

But I am also keeping an eye on what is going on beside me. By the time the movie is half over, Dad has his arm around Miss Isobel and she is leaning against him.

I remember when he used to sit like that with Mom. It makes me sad to think of that, but I am also a little bit glad for him.

When the movie is over, Dad tells me it's time for bed.

"Thank you for letting me share the evening with you, Garnet," Miss Isobel says.

I curtsy.

Dad hugs me. As I go to my room, they are cleaning up.

When I get up, Dad is sitting at the kitchen table, drinking coffee.

He looks serious, and I wonder if I have done something wrong. When I sit down, he says, "I've been thinking, Amber."

"Uh-oh," I say.

He chuckles, but then gets serious again. "You were right. I should have told you in advance that Isobel was going to join us last night. I'm sorry I didn't."

I blink. I am not used to Dad apologiz-
ing without me getting mad at him first.

He takes a sip of his coffee, then says,
"But it was fun, wasn't it?"

I smile at him. "Yep, it really was."

Chapter Fourteen

Dad gets lost taking me to the new house. "These places all look alike," he grumbles. "And so do these curvy streets."

I want to help him, but I'm lost too. And he's right about the houses. . . . . I've already seen three that I thought were mine, but weren't. After some wandering around, he punches the address into his GPS. It turns out we were only two blocks away.

When we pull into the driveway, Dad gives me a kiss and says, "See you next weekend."

Part of me would like him to see the inside of where I live now, but I can tell he doesn't want to. And I'm pretty sure Mom and Max don't want him to come in yet.

I wish we had some ritual for saying good-bye. I think we're going to need it now that I'm in the new house. That will be my job. . . . . Dad doesn't think of that kind of thing.

I'm feeling like one of those math problems from the practice tests. Amber traveled x miles from her dad's house and is back with her mom and her new stepfather. How many different emotions does Amber have now?

But my life is not a math problem, and my feelings aren't numbers.

I watch as Dad pulls out of the driveway.

When I go inside, I am amazed. It's starting to look like home. Mom and Max have done a lot of work over the weekend. Max grins when he sees me. "Glad you're back, Amber! Your mom is in the kitchen. . . . . You've got to see it."

Mom is at the kitchen table with a cup of tea. She looks more relaxed than I've seen her in a long time. And there's not a box in sight.

"Welcome back, honey. Did you have a nice weekend?"

"Except for Saturday Academy it was great," I say. I decide not to tell her about Miss Isobel.

"Let me give you a tour of the cabinets."

This is not as interesting as she thinks. However, I realize it is important. I always used to know where the cereal was and how to find a spoon. Now I have to learn all over again.

When I go up to my room, I see that the ceramic plaque Mom and Max made

for me is on the door. It says AMBER BROWN'S ROOM and has cartoon pictures of the three of us, along with a beautiful rainbow. I love this plaque.

"Max put it up," Mom says. "He thought it might help you feel at home."

My room is still piled high with boxes. It is definitely not looking like home yet.

Mom comes in. "I know you didn't have much time before you had to go to your dad's for the weekend, Amber, but you've really got to get started on your unpacking. Would you like some help?"

I decide I would.

We look for the box that Kelly labeled AMBER'S TREASURES. It's the most important one, and my room definitely won't feel right until my favorite things are out where I can see them.

Despite the label, the movers managed to put the treasure box at the bottom of a stack. Good thing it was sturdy.

We open it. Right on top is the box with the chewing gum ball.

Mom sighs. "I had hoped the movers might lose this."

"Not funny. And it's not going in the closet." I lift the box and talk to the ball directly. "Chewing gum ball, in this new house you have a place of honor on the shelf."

"You are a very strange child," Mom tells me.

"That's part of why you like me," I reply.

Mom pulls out the good-luck troll Aunt Pam sent me to help get through math tests. I like him, even though he is not very effective.

Next is the pig-taking-a-bubble-bath alarm clock/bank.

"This is getting heavy," Mom says. She sounds a little surprised.

It goes beside my bed. Gorilla is already on the bed. He did not get packed. . . . . I carried him here personally. Now the rest of the stuffed toys join him.

"Pizza's here!" Max calls.

Mom and I head downstairs.

Max is smiling. "Our first pizza from the new place! Don't worry, Amber, I told them to hold the anchovies."

Max and I pinch our fingers together as if we are holding wiggly anchovies. This is something Justin and I always did, and I taught it to Max.

We eat on the new plates. I like them.

I do not like the pizza.

I make a face and say, "This tastes wrong. It's not like from the old place."

"It's perfectly fine," Mom says.

How does she know if it tastes fine to me? Pizza is a very personal thing, and it is very important to me since it is my favorite food group.

"There's another pizzeria nearby," Max says. "We can try that one next week."

Back in my room, I make my way through the boxes to my bed. The pizza situation is really bothering me.

I start making a list of things I don't like about this new house.

1. *Pizza tastes funny*
2. *Don't know where anything is*
3. *Don't know my neighbors*

I stop. I suddenly realize this is going to be a big problem when Halloween comes. It took Justin and me years to map out the best route in our old neighborhood.

I add that to my list:

4. *Don't know who gives out best Halloween candy*
5. *My room has too many boxes in it*

All right, I know it's full of boxes because I haven't unpacked them yet. But secretly I also know that when I do unpack, it will mean that I really, really, really have moved here. I don't think I'm ready to face that.

I wrap my arms around Gorilla. He and I both refuse to open one more box.

Chapter Fifteen

Mom is standing in my doorway, looking cranky. "Amber, you've really got to finish unpacking. I understood you being tired on Sunday, but it's Thursday now and you've hardly begun. Even if it isn't bothering you, it's driving me slightly nuts. Every time I see all these boxes, it makes me feel like we're still moving in."

I don't want to admit it, but the boxes are starting to drive me slightly nuts too.

"Come on," Mom says. "Unpacking is better than packing. For one thing, I'm not asking you to throw anything away."

"Okay. But I want to do it myself."

I actually don't like the fact that I wasn't around for the kitchen unpacking because I'm still having trouble finding things. In my room I want to know where everything is.

Mom helps me cut open the boxes, and I get started.

It turns out unpacking is not as bad as I thought. The books are easy. I like putting them on the shelves and there's even room for new ones . . . . . . which I didn't have at the old house.

It turns out that unpacking is like eating peanuts . . . . . once you get started, it's hard to stop. I actually manage to empty every box.

By the time I am done, I'm pretty grubby.

One thing I definitely do like about our new house is that I have my own bathroom. Or maybe it should be called a shower room because it does not have a bathtub, just a shower. It is a tile stall with a glass door.

It's definitely time to degrub myself.

I get in and turn on the water. Looking out through the glass door makes me feel like I am in an aquarium. I've been worrying about being at the bottom of the aquarium. But actually I kind of like aquariums.

I wonder what it would be like to live in a real one. What kind of fish would I be? Not an angelfish. Not a guppy. Not a goldfish. Oh, I know. An Amberfish!

An Amberfish will need more water. I wonder if it is possible to fill the shower like an aquarium.

I sit on the drain to find out. This will be an experiment.

The water starts to rise. It's working!

I am feeling very scientific.

Of course, I can't fill the whole shower because then I would end up totally underwater. I decide I will stop when the water gets up to my waist.

I wonder how long that will take.

That makes me wish I had brought in a clock. Of course, it would have to be a waterproof clock.

I decide to count instead. I know that adding the word *Mississippi* to a number is a good way to count seconds.

Mississippi feels like a good word to add since I am sitting in water.

I close my eyes and start to count. I do not count for long. Instead, I start thinking about the Mississippi River. What kind of fish would I, Amberfish, meet in the Mississippi? Would I be able to teach them to spell M-I-S-S-I-S-S-I-P-P-I?

The water is getting higher. I am feeling very clever for having thought of this.

That feeling ends when Mom flings open the bathroom door and screams, "Amber, what's going on up here? There's water coming through the kitchen ceiling!"

I scramble to my feet and turn off the shower.

My experiment is going down the drain.

Mom is standing at the shower door. She has a horrified look on her face. When the water is below the edge of the door, she pulls the door open and hands me a towel.

Then she turns and runs back down the stairs.

I hear Max yelling. He is using words I have never heard from him before.

I wrap the towel around myself. I am terrified to see what is happening, but I know I have to find out.

When Mom and I go into the kitchen, I see Max staring at the ceiling. I look up and see a stain that was not there when I went upstairs. Even worse, it is dripping.

There is a puddle on the table. What's

left of the pizza is sitting in the middle
of it.

Max turns to us and says, "What happened? Did a pipe break?"

Mom looks at me.

I can feel myself blushing. "I was taking
a shower," I say.

"I'm calling the broker," Max says,
getting to his feet. "If there's something

wrong with the shower, it's the builder's fault and they'll have to pay for it."

Mom coughs. "I don't think there's anything wrong with Amber's shower."

Max stares at me.

I wish I could imitate the water and go through the floor. That doesn't happen.

"I was doing an experiment," I say at last.

"An experiment?"

"I wanted to see if the shower could be an aquarium."

"What were you doing, sitting on the drain?"

I don't answer. I don't have to. My face tells him that he got it right.

Max starts to say something, then closes his mouth. He points to the ceiling. His mouth opens again, but he snaps it closed.

"Max," Mom says, "it's not such a big deal."

"Not a big deal? If we hadn't been

sitting here, the whole ceiling might have come down before we knew what was happening!"

"I'm sorry," I say.

Max flings down the towel he was holding and stomps out of the room. We hear the front door open and slam shut.

I start to cry.

"Go to bed, Amber," Mom says. She doesn't tell me that everything is going to be all right.

I go upstairs.

I go to bed . . . . . but I do not go to sleep.

I, Amber Brown, have made more than one mistake in my life. But this may be my biggest mess ever.

Chapter Sixteen

When I go downstairs in the morning, Max is sitting in the kitchen, staring up at the ceiling. I look up and swallow. I had hoped that when the ceiling dried out, the stain would go away. It didn't . . . . . it is bigger than ever.

Even worse, the ceiling is starting to bulge.

"Morning," Max says.

I notice he does not say "Good morning." Also, he is not cheerful the way he usually is.

"I put Cheerios, milk, and a banana out on the counter for you. I don't want you sitting at the kitchen table . . . . some of that ceiling might come down at any time."

"Where's Mom?"

"She's getting ready to drive you to school."

He's still staring at the ceiling.

It's like he doesn't want to look at me because if he does, all he'll see is the leak.

I pour myself some cereal, but I do not eat much of it. My stomach is in no mood for it.

Mom comes into the kitchen. "Let's go, Amber."

We get in the car.

"Max is really mad at me, isn't he?" I say.

"He'll get over it," Mom tells me.

That must mean that he really is mad because otherwise he would not have to get over it. I want to ask what time he came back last night, but I'm not sure that's a good idea.

Mom sighs. "It's just that this is Max's first house, Amber, and he is so proud of it. He's really upset that something like this happened when we'd only been here for a week. I know you didn't mean to do it, but honestly, sitting on the drain was a foolish thing to do."

I know that now. I just wish I had known it last night!

I also realize that it was so foolish I don't want to tell anyone else about it, not even Kelly and Brandi. I don't want anyone to know I did something so dumb.

I'm so distracted that I keep messing up in the dance lessons that afternoon.

Finally Bobby says, "What's the problem, Amber? You were starting to get this step last week. Now it's like your head is somewhere else."

I do not, do not want to tell Bobby Clifford of all people that I sat on the shower drain and almost flooded our new kitchen. I know I will be called Leak Freak for the rest of the year . . . . . or maybe the rest of my life.

But I do feel like I need to talk to somebody. I wonder if I can tell Dad about it.

As it turns out, I don't have much chance to talk to him at all that night. That's because when we are walking to his car after school, he says, "Guess what?"

I am not in the mood for guessing games.

Dad does not notice. "We are making Friday movie night a party this week. Isobel is cooking a big dinner and the Marshall clan is coming down to join us."

I wish Dad had asked me if I thought this was a good idea or not. But before I can say that, Miss Isobel joins us. Like last week, her car is parked right next to Dad's. "This will be much fun," she says. "Good friends, good food, good talk. This is what life is all about, Carnelian."

When we get to Dad's house, I notice that Miss Isobel doesn't bring in any cooking equipment like she did the last time. In fact, Dad's kitchen is filled with things I've never seen before.

"What's that?" I ask, pointing to a ceramic thing that has beautiful designs on the outside and is shaped like an upside-down funnel.

"It is a tagine pot. I brought it home from Morocco, Sapphire."

"You do know my name is Amber, right?"

Miss Isobel laughs. "I know only that you are the jewel of your father's eye. You are precious in his sight, so every gem seems right for your name."

I feel better than I have all day. I'm sure not precious in Max's eyes right now. If Miss Isobel gave me a name based on how Max feels about me, it would probably be Mud.

I don't want to think about that right now, so I say, "Can I do anything to help, Miss Isobel?"

She looks at me. "How about at school

I am Miss Isobel, but when we are with your dad, you simply call me Isobel. And yes, you can help. The tagine is all made, but there are many finishing touches for us to do before dinner is ready."

Just then the Marshalls come through the door. There are four of them . . . . . Steve, who is the dad, then Polly, who is in high school, Dylan, who is in sixth grade, and Savannah, who is a year younger than me.

The tagine is delicious. . . . . . . It's a mix of chicken and vegetables and fruit that have cooked together for a long time. Even Dylan, whose basic food group, like mine, is pizza, asks for seconds. And then thirds.

Everybody helps with the cleanup, so it goes really fast. Then we watch *The Band Wagon*. Dylan gets a little disgusted by the mushy parts, but when three of the stars

dress in baby bonnets and sing about being triplets who "hate each other very much," it's so funny that we watch the song three times in a row.

It's a wonderful night. There is only one problem. I didn't need a party. I needed to be alone with my dad to talk. But by the time everyone has left, I am way too tired to tell him about the leak.

When I go to bed, I stare at the ceiling, which is not bulging. As I keep staring, I wonder how to make things right with Max. Then I realize it's probably not a good idea to talk to Dad about Max being so mad at me. It might just make things worse.

I am more confused than ever. Which may be why I don't do very well at Saturday Academy the next day.

Mr. Poindexter tells me that my practice tests are getting better. "Better, but not yet good enough. This is our last time together. You will need to focus intensely when you are taking the tests next week, Amber. And remember the things I told you about *how* to take a test."

Dad is alone when he comes to pick me up.

"Where is Miss Isobel?" I ask.

"She's at her studio, giving some lessons. I thought we could go to the park for a while, just take a walk. It's such a beautiful day."

I like this idea. And while we are walking, I get another idea. I won't tell Dad about my problems at home, but maybe I can still get some advice from him.

"You know those dad lessons you've been taking?" I say.

He smiles. "Well, yeah, I can hardly forget since I go every week."

"What kind of things do you talk about?"

He shrugs. "Life stuff. How to do better with people. How to be a better person. And, of course, how to be a better dad."

"Do you ever talk about what to do when you've hurt someone or made a bad mistake?"

Dad looks at me curiously. I can tell he really wants to ask if something has happened. Instead he just says, "My counselor has told me the first thing to do is admit that I screwed up. But she also says that just saying you're sorry isn't enough. It's better if you can show that you're sorry and then try to figure out a way to make things better. Sometimes it doesn't happen fast. Think of the times you've been so mad at me."

I do. And then I think of the fact that I've never stopped loving Dad and feeling that he loves me back.

I need to do something to show Max that I am sorry.

It's not until I am going to sleep that night that I finally figure out what it's going to be.

Chapter
Seventeen

I, Amber Brown, am sitting in my room. Mom and Max are out working in the yard.

Mom seemed happy to see me. Max acted like he was happy to see me, but he is not a very good actor.

I am sitting at my desk. Beside me is the pig-taking-a-bubble-bath alarm clock/bank that Aunt Pam gave me.

I write a note. I don't use glitter. I don't use fancy paper. I keep it simple.

Dear Max,

Please use the money in this bank to help repair the ceiling. I am very sorry for what I did, and I hope you will forgive me. I know you are proud of this new house, and I feel very bad that I created such a mess.

Love,
Amber

I take my note and the bank down to the kitchen. I put it on the counter. Then I go back to my room.

I lie down on my bed and start to cry. I am leaking worse than the ceiling. I am not trying to get attention. I am not trying to get sympathy. I just can't hold it in anymore.

Even though I thought I was being quiet, Mom comes in.

"Amber, what is it?" she asks.

I just shake my head. I can't answer her. She holds out her arms. I sit up and put my head against her chest.

She rocks me for a while, then says, "Amber, tell me about it."

"It's not it," I sob. "It's everything."

It all comes out . . . . . how upset I am about the move . . . . how worried I am about the tests . . . . . . and most of all, how bad I feel about what I did to the house.

"I think Max hates me," I sob.

"I don't," says a quiet voice.

I look up. Max is standing in the doorway.

He comes into the room and sits on the floor next to the bed.

"I appreciate your apology, Amber. I could tell it came from your heart, and it made me feel better. But it made me realize that I also owe you an apology. I was really mad about what happened . . . . . too mad. I got so upset about the house that I lost track of the fact that what I really wanted is a home . . . . . a home with you and your mother, the people I love. I got kind of trapped by my anger, and I should have moved on by now. I'm sorry."

For a little while, no one says anything. Then Max stands up.

"Can I have a hug?" he asks softly.

I stand up. So does Mom. We all hold each other close.

Maybe this place can be home after all. . . .

Chapter Eighteen

Testing is weird. The whole school feels different . . . . . especially our classroom. It's usually so colorful. Now the walls are bare!

"What happened to this place?" Jimmy Russell asks. "A sneak attack from the bulletin board bandit?"

Mrs. Holt shakes her head. "State testing rules mandate that our room can't have anything displaying words or numbers on the walls while testing is taking place."

"Why?" Brandi asks. "Are they afraid

you're going to post the answers on the walls?"

Mrs. Holt gives her a weak smile and says, "Ours is not to reason why, ours is but to test and try."

I think she's mangling an old poem, but I'm not sure.

Once everyone is in their seats and the room is quiet, she says, "All right, you all know the drill. In a minute I will pass out the test booklets and the number two pencils. Remember, you must not use anything other than the pencil I give you."

"You mean we all have to do number two?" Bobby cries.

A few kids laugh. I want to laugh too, but I think it's probably not a good idea.

Hannah Burton rolls her eyes and says, "You are so gross, Bobby!"

To my surprise, Mrs. Holt doesn't say anything. Instead, she walks over to Bobby's desk and stares at him. Everyone is quiet now. The silence goes on for a long time.

Finally Bobby says, "Sorry, Mrs. Holt," in a very quiet voice.

Mrs. Holt nods and goes back to the front of the room. "Remember, class . . . . the machines that score these tests aren't as smart as you are. They can't read anything but a number two pencil."

We laugh, but it's not a very easy laugh.

"I'm going to pass the booklets out now, but don't open them yet. The state mandates that before you do, I must read you the instructions word for word. All right, before we officially start, everybody take a deep breath. Let it out. Smile."

If my smile looks like the ones around me, we could label a photograph of us NOTHING TO SMILE ABOUT.

I get my booklet.

Mrs. Holt reads us the instructions.

We begin.

I know you are supposed to focus when you are taking the tests, but the people who give them don't seem to realize that sometimes your life has other things going on that distract you.

I am glad that things have settled down at home. Otherwise I do not think there would have been any point in me taking the tests at all. But today I am ready to focus.

I don't think about missing my old house.

I don't think about the leak.

I don't think about how much I wish I was outside doing something else.

I think about sticking to the path. For each question I try to figure out what the test is really asking.

I pretend I am a camera. I can only take one picture at a time. Each question is a picture and I have to focus on it and nothing else.

Some of the questions are very easy. Some don't make any sense at all. I know I do not have to get them all right. . . . . . . Mr. Poindexter told us that we are not even expected to get them all right.

Before Saturday Academy, I used to worry about that a lot. I would get stuck on a question and it would get me so upset that I couldn't move on to the next. Today

I do the best I can, then pick an answer and go on.

Mrs. Holt walks around the room. She can't talk to us, but she's not allowed to sit down either. You would think the people who make these rules would know how distracting that is.

Thinking about that makes me start to think about how silly some of these rules are. If I were in charge of the tests, I would make different rules.

Yikes! I have totally lost my focus.

I take a deep breath and bring myself back to the path . . . . back to the test.

This feels different. Maybe part of focusing is learning to know when you've left the path and making sure you get back on it.

I move on to the next question. And the next.

All the way to the end of the test.

Chapter Nineteen

"All right, ladies and gentlemen, it's time for the swing. Take your positions. Ready? Five, six, seven, eight, dance!"

The crowd begins to yell. I know that Mom and Max are watching. And Dad. And Mrs. Holt. And Miss Isobel, and even Ramón. I know, but I don't fuss about it.

Bobby and I bounce to the beat of the music. In swing you're supposed to smile, and Bobby and I are both grinning. I keep my eyes on him and we don't miss a step.

Before the contest started . . . . . and even through the first couple of dances . . . . I had butterflies in my stomach. Now I feel like I've got wings on my shoulders.

Miss Isobel taught us that the swing is a dance where we should let loose and yet remain in control. That never made sense to me before, but suddenly that's what Bobby and I are doing.

The judges move around the dance floor, tapping the shoulders of other couples. When they tap your shoulder, you are out.

During the tango, we were one of the first couples to get tapped. Brandi and Fredrich won that one. I've never seen Fredrich look so happy.

Bobby and I didn't do that well in the waltz or the fox trot either.

Swing wasn't even a dance we thought we were good at. But suddenly we are flying.

Now there are only three couples left.

My legs are feeling like jelly. I don't think we've ever danced this long.

Bobby begins to laugh.

I do too.

I hope we win.

Even if we don't, I know that I, Amber Brown, will keep dancing . . . . . and keep moving on.

TURN THE PAGE FOR A LOOK AT

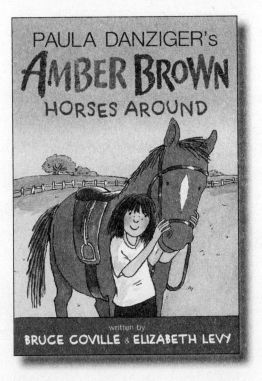

PAULA DANZIGER's
AMBER BROWN
HORSES AROUND

written by
BRUCE COVILLE & ELIZABETH LEVY

Chapter One

I, Amber Brown, am one happy camper.

This is a strange thing to say, because I have never been at camp . . . . . and I am not there now! Even so, I am a happy camper because I made it through fourth grade and tomorrow I am heading for Camp Cushetunk.

That's the good news.

The bad news is that first I have to pack.

I hate packing. There are too many choices to make!

I am looking at the pile of stuff on my

bed when Mom and Max knock on my door.

I know it is both of them, because the door is open.

I have trained them to knock even when it is.

Max is my new stepfather. I was kind of rotten to him when he started to go out with Mom, but I kind of love him now.

"Come in," I say.

Mom is carrying the packing list that the camp sent. I like lists. I especially like this one because there is a little box next to each item that you can check when you've taken care of it. This is very satisfying.

However, the list is missing things like "Gorilla" and "pig-taking-a-bubble-bath alarm clock/bank." I think I have to leave those things at home. Not because I don't want to have them with me . . . . it's

just that I don't want the other campers to make fun of me for bringing them.

Sometimes it's hard to figure out what is too baby and what is all right.

Max holds up a plastic bag. "I just went to the drugstore, Amber. I think I got everything we still needed."

I thought I liked lists, but I am nothing compared to Max. He LOVES lists.

He also loves labels. I think maybe the two things go together. He has had a fine time ironing name tags onto my shirts and shorts.

I didn't let him do my underwear. I made Mom do that.

When I asked Max how he got so handy with an iron, he explained that it was a side effect of living alone for so many years.

Max starts to unpack the drugstore bag. He holds up a toothbrush. "You're going to love this, Amber. It's got a timer inside and it lights up after you've brushed for two minutes."

Two minutes is how long the dentist wants me to brush, but I usually get bored before two minutes go by. The light is very cool.

Mom says, "Why don't you go grab Amber's towels, Max."

While he is gone, she picks up one of my T-shirts and looks at the name tag. "Amber Brown. I love that I gave you such a colorful name."

I love my name too. But I don't love that Mom's last name is no longer Brown. When she got married to Max, it became Turner.

Max comes back in and puts a stack of towels on the bed. Then he goes to my desk. "Make sure everything has a name tag on it before you pack it."

"I don't think the camp really meant

everything," Mom says. "No one puts a name tag on a tube of toothpaste."

I look at Max and start to laugh. He has a tube of toothpaste in one hand and a fine-point Sharpie in the other. He drops the Sharpie and tries to pretend he wasn't about to label my toothpaste.

"Busted!" I say.

Mom sighs. "Oh, Max. Next thing you know, you'll be labeling her sticks of gum!"

I can't tell whether she is amused or exasperated.

When the trunk is packed, they go downstairs.

"Don't forget we're leaving for the airport in fifteen minutes," Mom calls over her shoulder.

Tonight, Justin Daniels, my very best friend ever, is flying up from Alabama. He is going to Cushetunk too! This is the best, best, best thing ever.

The reason it is the best, best, best thing ever is that I almost never get to see Justin anymore. That's because of one of the worst, worst, worst things ever . . . . his parents moved to Alabama! I thought they should leave Justin behind so we could keep going to school together, but they refused.

Now we're going to be at camp together for four whole weeks. The idea is so exciting, I am afraid my head will explode before we even leave for the airport to get Justin.

I decide to check my e-mail, just to try to keep my head in one piece while I am waiting. I have only had e-mail for a few days . . . . . it was a reward for graduating from fourth grade.

My e-mail name is "Notacrayon."

When I open the account, I see that there is a message from Brandi Colwin. It is addressed to me and Kelly Green.

7

This is another reason I am so sure Camp Cushetunk will be wonderful. Brandi and Kelly are my best friends from school, and they are going too. It should be great!

Brandi's subject line is "Bulletin! Bulletin! Bulletin!"

She is practicing to be a newscaster, and this is her way of letting Kelly and me know that she has something important to tell us.

I open the e-mail, and groan.

Chapter Two

I don't watch the news that much, but I see it more often now that Max is with us. And something I've noticed is that most of the news is bad.

Brandi's e-mail is definitely something that belongs on the bad news channel.

OMG! I JUST FOUND OUT THAT
HANNAH BURTON IS GOING TO
CAMP CUSHETUNK!!

I want to beat my head against the key-board. Hannah and I have been in school

9

together forever, and we have never liked each other.

Hannah Burton is tinfoil on your teeth . . . . . . itching powder down your back . . . . . . a giant booger in your soup.

"What if we're in a bunk with her?" I e-mail back.

Before Brandi can answer, Max calls, "Time to go to the airport!"

I am out of my chair, down the stairs, and into the car while Mom and Max are still getting their things together.

"I checked the flight," Max says as he climbs into the driver's seat. "It's right on time."

It feels like the airport is a million miles away. Every stop sign and traffic light makes me want to scream. I want to be there NOW.

Mom and Max are yakking away like this is just a normal ride. I realize they are talking about the movies they want to see while I am gone. I am not sure I like this . . . . . I think they should just stay home and miss me. I know that is silly, but I can't always control how I feel about things.

When we finally get to the airport, we have to walk a billion zillion miles from the parking garage to where we are supposed to meet Justin. Because he is a kid traveling alone, one of the airplane people will walk him out to us.

I see him! But he is not looking for me. He is chatting away to the woman walking beside him. She is in a uniform and looks very official. She is also very beautiful. For some reason I find this very annoying.

Suddenly he turns in our direction. "Amber!" he cries, and runs toward me. Just like when he came up for Mom and Max's wedding, we almost hug, and then stop.

I look at him. His hair has gotten longer, and he is even more tan than the last
time I saw him. But he is still Justin. Then
he smiles, and I see the big change. He has
braces!

"This is Ms. Block," Justin says. "She's
in training to be a pilot."

Ms. Block shakes hands with Mom and
Max and asks them for ID to make sure
we are the people who are supposed to

pick up Justin. Mom thanks her, and Ms. Block walks away. Justin watches her go.

I tap him on the shoulder. He turns back to me and says, "I think I want to be a pilot when I grow up."

"Come on, flyboy," Max says. "We need to get your luggage."

"Was it scary traveling alone?" I ask Justin.

"No, it was kind of fun. Except they almost paid too much attention to me. But I had my own little TV set. That was cool!"

The luggage comes out on something called a carousel, which would make you think it was like a merry-go-round because it does go around and around. But there aren't any horses. It's a big oval that carries the suitcases and backpacks past the people waiting to claim them. I soooooo want to climb onto it and take a ride . . . . . . I bet it would be fun.

This is when I realize that Max is getting to know me a little too well. He looks down at me and says firmly, "Don't even think about it!"

"That's mine!" Justin says, pointing to a big trunk.

Max hauls it off the carousel. "Ooof! What did you pack in here? Your little brother?"

"I hope he's not in there!" Justin says. "One of the reasons I wanted to go to camp was to get away from him!"

We laugh and head for the car.